# Silent Harvest

## A Christmas in the E.R. Thriller

## Kristina Fox

Self-Published

# Contents

# Chapter 1

2009

A rush of energy slurred into the room as EMTs wheeled two gurneys in. The man bled profusely from his neck despite the EMTs' efforts to hold pressure. The woman, whose wounds seemed to be superficial, was fading in and out of consciousness.

"We've got a thirty-five-year-old male, car accident, no seatbelt. Windshield cut his throat. We found him six feet away from the car. Trachea is intact, but the carotid is nicked."

"Prep OR 3, and someone page Dr. Adler," Nurse Molly Fisher called out as she guided the gurney toward the elevator.

"Already done," Physician's Assistant Art Chin said as he slipped into the elevator with Molly and the EMT. "Dr. Adler will meet us in the O.R."

On the way up to the operating room, they continued to apply pressure to the man's neck. Molly looked up and recognized the emergency technician as her friend Luke Sims. She had known Luke for the past two years. They lived in the same apartment building and saw one another in passing from time to time. She threw a nod in his direction.

"Well, hello to you, too, Miss Molly," Luke said.

"Do we have a name for him, Luke? Any ID?"

Molly was all business when it came to saving lives; her usual spunky personality became rigid and stoic.

"Yep, Jose Torres. The woman we brought in is his girlfriend, twenty-three-year-old Antonia Lopez," Luke said. "We had to extract her from the car, but she's in much better condition than he is. In the ambulance, Mr. Torres asked us to call his wife."

"His wife? I thought you said the woman was his girlfriend," Molly said, confused.

Luke shrugged. "That's what she told us."

"Mr. Torres? Mr. Torres?" Molly said. "My name is Nurse Fisher. We're going to help you, okay? I need you to keep your eyes open for me. Don't try to speak. Blink once if you understand."

The man on the stretcher looked up at Molly, fear in his eyes. He knew he was dying. He felt the life start to leave his body. The shadows on the elevator ceiling pressed down on his body, trying to suffocate him. The nurse was speaking to him, but he couldn't understand what she was saying. Her lips were moving, but no sound came from them. His eyelids were so heavy. It was impossible to keep them open any longer.

"Molly, scrub in," Dr. Adler called from inside the operating room. Luke wheeled the patient into the room, and the nurses transferred the man onto the table.

"Later, alligator," Luke said, rushing past Molly and back into the elevator.

Butterflies fluttered in Molly's belly as she entered the O.R. This was the fourth surgery that she would be assisting Dr. Adler with.

It was an honor to work alongside him. Recognized as one of the top trauma surgeons in the San Diego area, Dr. Adler held numerous awards for saving lives in the community.

"Okay, Molly, I need you to take over holding pressure. Art, we're going to need more blood. Get me three units of O-positive," Dr. Adler said.

"Yes, Doctor," Art said, scrambling out the door.

"Blood pressure dropping," Molly said. "85 over 60."

Dr. Adler sutured the man's carotid artery as Molly suctioned the blood filling the cavity. The stitches were clean and tight; however, the man's cavity filled with more blood.

"Shit. Where is all this blood coming from? Can you see it?"

Molly used the suction to clear more blood. Dr. Adler pushed the carotid artery aside to find where the bleeding was coming from.

"There!" Molly said. "There's a puncture wound. Medial aspect of the internal jugular."

Every machine in the room started blaring.

"Patient's coding!" Dr. Adler said as he held the jugular together. "Trish, get me an 8-0 nylon on a vascular needle. Molly, clamp."

Dr. Adler reached for the resuscitation paddles and placed them on the patient.

"Clear!"

The patient's body jolted back to life. Without skipping a beat, Dr. Adler slid the needle into the vein.

"Where's Art with the blood?" he said.

"I'm here!" Art rushed into the room, moving quickly to set up the blood tubing.

In a matter of seconds, the machines stopped beeping, and the patient's blood pressure started to stabilize. Dr. Adler finished suturing the vein and the patient's neck. Molly and Trish rolled Jose to the ICU unit, where he would be carefully monitored by staff.

"That was a close one," Trish said, taking her gloves and gown off.

"No kidding. There was so much blood, I was surprised the guy had any left," Molly said. "Art made it just in time. I sure am glad my shift is over. Time for a nice hot bubble bath."

As she made her way to the front desk, Molly observed the hospital's other trauma surgeon, Bradley Mills, walking through the double doors. Their eyes met, and he acknowledged her with a tip of his chin.

"Hello, Nurse Fisher," he said.

"Afternoon, Dr. Mills," she responded.

Although Molly had never worked the same shift as Dr. Mills, from what she had heard through the grapevine, he was unpleasant to work with, belittling the nurses and other hospital staff. Dr. Adler was the complete opposite. He was kind, respectful, and professional.

# Chapter 2

"HE WHAT?" MOLLY ASKED in disbelief.

"He died last night," Trish told her.

Molly sat with her head in her hands. She felt like crying.

"I can't believe it. What happened?"

"They're not sure yet. ICU nurses said that he started hemorrhaging and they couldn't control the bleeding. The police are opening up an investigation into it," Trish said.

"What happened to the girlfriend who came in with him?" Molly said.

"She was discharged yesterday with a few bumps and bruises," Trish said.

"So, she left? Did they ever reach his wife?"

"Mm, hmm. The girlfriend left in a rush. Not a word after she was discharged. Mr. Torres' wife arrived as soon as she received the news. They have a three-year-old son."

Molly shook her head. "That poor woman. I wonder if she knew about the girlfriend."

"It's awful," Trish said. "This is the second patient this month who has passed under very odd circumstances."

"Right. The first was the man who came in so disoriented that we thought he was drunk. Slurred words and in and out of consciousness. His roommate brought him in. Phenobarbital. The guy's levels were through the roof. He had already gone into respiratory and circulatory collapse. Dr. Adler intubated and administered noradrenaline and charcoal, but the patient died within an hour."

"Hmm. Did they think it was under suspicious circumstances?" Trish asked.

"No, but if you ask me, it seems like a possible poisoning rather than an overdose," Molly said.

"Because of the levels?" Trish asked.

"That, and don't say anything, but his roommate seemed a little too calm for the situation. And get this, the patient was a convicted pedophile who had been on the national news several times," Molly said.

"Oh, wow," Trish said, at a loss for words. "So, you think the roommate killed him?"

"The roommate, a friend, sure. The timeline the roommate gave us was fuzzy."

"Weird that he didn't react differently, too," Trish added.

"Agreed. Although it could have been because the roommate is a nurse right here in this hospital."

Trish looked at Molly for a second before asking, "Who was it?"

"An ICU nurse."

# Chapter 3

THE WINTER AIR CHILLED Molly's cheeks as she, her best friend, Rachel, and Rachel's five-year-old son, Patrick, warmed their hands on cups of hot cocoa. The downtown area was bustling with families getting ready for the holiday season. Rachel stopped to admire the front window of her favorite boutique, Ginger and Lou. In it, a small toy train puffed around a circular track. In the middle sat a miniature Christmas tree adorned with handmade ornaments.

"Ooh, can we go in here, Mama?" Patrick said. "Can we?"

"I think that's a great idea," Molly said.

Rachel was like a little girl in a candy store, her eyes wide, as she took in all the sparkles and shimmer.

"Hello, ladies and young man! Welcome to Ginger and Lou's. What brings you in?" a cheerful lady greeted them.

"I love this store. My mama used to bring me in here when I was wee high," Rachel said, hovering her hand three feet from the floor. "Every birthday, Christmas, and sometimes just because."

A tear formed in Rachel's eye. She wiped it away, her eyes reddening. "Sorry. She passed three years ago. Cancer."

"Oh, dear. I'm so sorry," the woman said. "I understand. My grandmother opened this store back in 1970. I took over after she and my mother passed. I miss them both every day. But being here, I feel their energy in the store, and I know I'm not alone."

Rachel nodded. "I think I feel it too."

"Me, too," Patrick said.

Molly wrapped her arm around her friend's shoulder. "How about we choose something for your tree this year?"

As they left the shop, Rachel turned to Molly and said, "Sorry about that. Crying in public is so not cool."

"Don't be sorry. I would be devastated if my mom died," Molly said.

"Speaking of your mom, how is she?"

"She's great. She has a new boyfriend, and I think things are getting hot and heavy. He's a great guy from what she tells me. My mom describes him as this big teddy bear who laughs like Santa Claus," Molly said.

"Aww, I'm so happy for your mom. She deserves a good life," Rachel said.

"Hey, so speaking of my mom, I've told you that one of our Christmas traditions is to make handmade ornaments for the tree each year. Last year, my mom made a mini nutcracker out of balsa wood. I tried my hand at crochet and made a snowman. This year, I was inspired to purchase a booth at the Christmas Bazaar. Do you two want to help me with it?"

Rachel's eyes lit up. "Would I? Oh, Molly, you know Christmas is my favorite holiday. Of course, we would love to help you. What do you think, Patrick?"

"Mm, hmm."

"I was hoping you'd say that," Molly said. "I was thinking we could do a craft and wine night at my place. Apple cider for you, buddy."

Molly crocheted all types of critters. She had seahorses, starfish, bumblebees, ladybugs, and a whole slew of Christmas-themed ornaments, including snowmen and Christmas trees. Her pride and joy, though, was a table display of Santa's sleigh, complete with Santa himself, his sack of presents, and, of course, his reindeer.

"Let's do it," Rachel said. "What's our next night off together?"

The two women checked their phones to compare schedules and planned to meet on the following Wednesday. As Molly slid her phone into her bag, a familiar voice spoke.

"Well, hello Nurse Fisher, Nurse Banks."

Molly looked up and saw Dr. Mills with a young, brunette woman on his arm. *That woman seems a little young for Dr. Mills*, Molly thought.

"Oh, hello, Dr. Mills," Molly said.

Rachel smiled and nodded at the doctor.

"This is my little sister, Margot. She's here visiting from the San Francisco Bay Area. We decided to spend Thanksgiving Day together, although I'm on call that evening. Any plans for the holiday, you two?"

Molly had never had a conversation with Dr. Mills before. Usually, they greeted one another in passing as a formality. As Molly looked up at Dr. Mills, about to formulate an answer, she realized how good-looking the man was.

# Chapter 4

"HE DID WHAT?" RACHEL said.

"He asked me to dinner."

"What did you say?"

"Uh, I said okay. I said yes," Molly said. "And before you say anything, I am fully aware of what the other nurses say about him."

"Be careful, Molly. This is your job we're talking about," Rachel said.

"Yes, Mom."

All afternoon, Molly replayed her conversation with Dr. Mills. She was so surprised when he called her. She was even more surprised when he asked her if she would like to accompany him to dinner at a friend's restaurant for a grand opening event. The restaurant was already creating buzz in the San Diego community, with food critics and influencers lining up to make reservations.

Molly accepted the invitation, although she wondered if he had an ulterior motive. They didn't know one another, after all. Not really.

"Molly, chest tube," Dr. Adler's voice brought Molly out of her stupor.

Molly handed him the tubing. An obese woman in her late sixties lay on the table, her lung collapsed. Her son had brought her in, saying that she was complaining of chest pain. She was also short of breath.

"Molly, can you ask the son what Mrs. Stephenson was doing at the time the chest pain started?"

Molly walked out to the waiting room, where the woman's son was pacing back and forth.

"Mr. Stephenson?" Molly asked.

"John. You can call me John," the young man said.

"The doctor would like to obtain a little more information about what happened when your mother started to feel chest pain. What was she doing when the symptoms started?"

"Sure, of course. If it'll help. My mom fell asleep in her favorite chair after dinner. She wears a CPAP at night while she sleeps because of her apnea, but when she falls asleep in her chair, I usually leave her there until she wakes up to go to bed. This time, she woke up gasping for air and clutching her chest. Is she going to be okay?"

"We're doing our best. She's with the doctor right now," Molly reassured John.

Molly rushed back to the trauma bay to give the information to Dr. Adler. As she entered the room, it was eerily silent. The woman's body was covered, and the machines were turned off.

"What? What happened?" Molly exclaimed.

Dr. Adler shook his head and said under his breath, "You know, Molly. Sometimes I don't feel sorry for people. It's my job to save their lives, but they sure don't make it easy. We can only do our best. Too bad Mrs. Stephenson here didn't value her life enough to lose the weight."

Molly wasn't sure what to make of the doctor's sudden proclamation, so she kept her mouth shut.

# Chapter 5

A CROWD GATHERED AT the front entrance to celebrate the opening of Fire & Fork Steakhouse, a much-anticipated addition to San Diego's culinary offerings. Owner Grady Morris and grill master Scotty O'Farrell stood outside behind the red satin ribbon. Mayor Jerry Sanders held an oversized pair of scissors, and with the clamoring of press and paparazzi, you would have thought an entourage of A-list celebrities was attending.

Dr. Bradley Mills had picked Molly up from her apartment, and Molly found the half-hour drive to the restaurant to be filled with pleasant conversation and even some laughs. Brad told her about Thanksgiving with his sister, and Molly told him about the Christmas Bazaar she and Rachel were getting ready for. Brad had been nothing but respectful to her so far, and she hoped it would stay that way. Although Molly was wearing a coat over her sweater dress, the chill in the air made her shiver. Brad took his wool overcoat off and slid it around her shoulders.

"Thank you," she said.

"My pleasure," he said, a warm smile spreading across his face.

As the owner, chef, and mayor each said a few words, Molly wondered when they would be seated. As if reading her mind, Brad whispered to her, "It should only be a few minutes. They like to make a big deal of these things. Trust me, Grady lives for this stuff."

Molly chuckled as Brad gave her a little smirk, putting his arm around her. Molly leaned into him, not only for warmth, but because having his arm around her felt right.

The evening went well, and the more she and Brad conversed, the more she recognized that they were not so different. Their love of helping people was a topic neither one could get enough of. Molly laughed as Brad described his years as a resident, and Brad was impressed as Molly told him about how she was raised by a single mother and put herself through nursing school.

At the end of the night, after devouring the most delicious Kobe beef and the restaurant's signature garlic-smashed potatoes, Brad asked her, "So, how do you like working with Todd?"

"You mean Dr. Adler?" Molly said, giggling from the wine.

Brad laughed and said, mimicking a serious tone, "Yes, Dr. Adler."

"Hmm, well, he's been nothing but professional when we've worked together. I'm impressed by his precision in surgery," Molly said.

Brad nodded.

"Have you worked with him before?" Molly asked.

"He was my mentor. I agree that Dr. Adler is a very skilled surgeon," Brad said, but there was something in his voice that lingered.

"But?" Molly asked.

Brad looked up at her. "Just an observation. Dr. Adler seems a little more rigid recently. For someone of his caliber, I'm unsure if he's been unlucky or if there's something else going on, but there aren't a lot of people coming in and dying from a collapsed lung. Usually, there's something more to it. I was only wondering if you noticed anything."

Molly looked at Brad in disbelief. Was he saying what she thought he was saying? Was he implying that Dr. Adler was killing his patients on purpose?

"I'm sorry, Molly," Brad said. "We shouldn't be talking about this. You seem to be his new favorite nurse, is all, so I thought I'd ask."

So, this is why he invited her out to dinner. The other nurses were right. What an asshole. He wanted information from her.

Molly took her napkin from her lap, neatly folded it, and placed it on the table beside her plate. She stood and said, "Thank you, Brad. Or maybe I should go back to calling you Dr. Mills. I had a lovely time, and this is a wonderful restaurant. Please thank your friend for me. I think it's time for me to go, though."

Molly couldn't believe she had been so stupid to think that a trauma surgeon might want to date her. She wasn't gorgeous like a supermodel, but she wasn't ugly by any means, and most people told her she had a warm, likable personality.

Brad stood up. "No, please, Molly. That's not what I meant. Please sit down. Let me explain."

Not wanting to make a scene, Molly sat back down.

"I didn't say yes to dinner so that you could probe me for information about Dr. Adler. And as for being his favorite nurse, I'm as hardworking as everyone else in that ER. I am grateful for every surgery that he asks me to assist him with. I'm not his favorite, and I don't kiss his ass."

"I wasn't trying to offend you. Can we please start over, Molly? I really like you. I've had more fun on this date than I've had in years. Please don't go."

Molly looked at Brad. The glimmer in his eyes looked like that of desperation and something else. She took a deep breath.

"I thought we were having fun, too. But I'm not okay with you or anyone asking me for gossip about Dr. Adler. Trish and Art also work closely with him, so it's not like we're ever alone. I'm not sure what you're getting at."

"It's nothing, okay? Just a hunch. Let's forget this part of the conversation. I'm sorry I made you uncomfortable."

Molly nodded, accepting Brad's apology and another pour of wine.

# Chapter 6

NOW THAT THANKSGIVING HAD come and gone, Molly and Brad made plans for the next holiday, Christmas. It was Molly's favorite holiday, and Brad admitted that he also had fond memories of Christmas growing up. They planned to go to Molly's mom's house for Christmas morning and spend the evening together making a home-cooked meal.

The Christmas Bazaar was bright and merry as vendors set up their goods. From baked goods to homemade crafts, the bazaar had it all. Molly and Rachel made three hundred and twenty-five handmade ornaments for Molly's table. The tablecloth Molly ordered on Etsy was hand-embroidered with the words "Molly's Merry Moments." Rachel came up with the name, and Molly loved the sound of it.

"No Patrick today?" Molly asked when Rachel came to pick her up.

"No, he said it was too cold outside."

Molly laughed. "It *is* pretty chilly out."

As Rachel organized the ornaments on the table, she said to Molly, "So, how's it going with Brad?"

Molly blushed at the sound of his name. "I like him. He's nothing like the rumors that are circulating about him."

"Hmm," Rachel answered. "What's he like?"

"He's kind and chivalrous. He's funny and helpful," Molly gushed.

"Sounds like Prince Charming. What do you guys talk about?" Rachel asked. "Work?"

Molly paused and looked at her best friend.

"Actually, no. He brought up work on our first date, and I accused him of probing me for information."

Rachel's eyes went wide. "What kind of information?"

"It was nothing. He asked how I liked working for Dr. Adler. It irked me that he said I was one of Dr. Adler's favorite nurses."

"What did you say? Did he ask you about specific patients?"

"No, no, nothing like that. I told him I don't want to talk about work when we're together. Brad and I have plenty of other things in common to talk about besides work," Molly said. "I'm going to check out the coffee stand. Want something?"

"Sure, I'll take a latte," Rachel answered. "And a scone. You know what I like."

Molly nodded and made her way toward the coffee stand. What was up with Rachel asking her questions about work? Rachel never did that. They had been friends in nursing school and agreed not to speak about what happened in the ER. Not only did it violate HIPAA laws, but some of the occurrences in the ER were too gruesome to rehash.

Molly returned with their snacks and coffee. She sat down next to Rachel.

"He's only thirty-two years old," Molly said. "Pretty impressive to be a trauma surgeon that young."

"I agree," Rachel said.

Rachel took a bite of her scone. "Ooh, oatmeal apricot. My favorite."

"Hi, ladies," Brad said. He was holding a steaming cup of coffee in his hand. "I would ask if you'd like coffee, but I see you've already made a trip over to the stand."

Molly stood and walked around the table to hug Brad. He kissed her on the cheek, making her blush. Molly looked at her watch.

"I thought you had to be at the hospital," she said.

"Not until eleven. I figured I'd stop by and say hello," Brad said. "How are sales going?"

"Three ornaments sold so far. I'm hoping people are planning to come at lunch for the Christmas play," Molly said.

"Well, I'm sure you'll be sold out by the end of the day," Brad said, picking up a whimsical frog ornament. "These critters will sell like hot cakes."

"Thanks for the vote of confidence," Molly said.

"Anytime," Brad said, winking at Molly, then bringing her in for a kiss.

Although they had only been dating for a few weeks, they had spent every day off together, a challenging feat for an ER trauma surgeon and nurse. Some evenings were cozy, snuggled up on the couch with Chinese takeout and a movie, and others were spent at fancy dinners and strolling around downtown San Diego. Molly found that it wasn't about what they did or where they went; it was about the company they kept. Brad made her feel safe.

# Chapter 7

MOLLY WATCHED AS HAPPY children and adults circled the outdoor skating rink, laughing and cheering. Couples were holding hands, and she longed to do the same with Brad. It was the most wonderful time of the year after all.

"Another four ornaments sold, Moll," Rachel said. "The teddy bears and butterflies are the most popular."

"I'll keep that in mind for next year," Molly said as she sipped on her third cup of coffee.

"I'm going to use the restroom," Rachel said. "Be right back."

"Sure. I'll hold the fort down," Molly said. She stood to straighten a few of the ornaments. A rush of customers came by that morning, and they all seemed to love Molly's crochet cuties. Rachel was right. She had made twenty teddy bears, and only six were left.

Molly's phone vibrated on the table, and she picked it up, hoping it was a message from Brad. Instead, it was a news alert:

**San Diego doctor murdered. Hospital on lockdown.**

Molly's heart sank into her stomach as her finger hovered over the link. There were at least ten hospitals in San Diego. The murdered doctor could be at any one of those hospitals, she told herself.

She scanned the article and jumped as Rachel said, "Hey, what's wrong? Are you okay? What are you reading?"

"Rach, it says a doctor was murdered at a hospital in San Diego. It doesn't say what hospital or what the doctor's name is. Only that it's under investigation."

"Oh, no. You don't think it's one of our doctors?" Rachel said, the color draining from her face. "Trish is working the desk today. Call her."

"Good idea," Molly said, her finger swiping up and bringing up the list of favorites on her phone. She clicked "Work."

The phone rang for what felt like an eternity. Rachel leaned over to listen in on the call, pressing herself against her friend. Molly's breaths were shallow as they waited. Grabbing Molly's hand, Rachel tried to reassure her friend and said, "I'm sure it'll be okay. It can't be our hospital. Someone would have called us by now."

"San Diego Hospital, can you please hold?" The voice on the line said.

Molly took an inflated breath and pushed it out. Rachel was right. That was Trish on the phone. Surely Trish would have sent her a text if something was wrong. The elevator music played on her phone, and a text came in. It was from Trish. Molly clicked on the notification.

*Dr. Mills was found dead in a supply room. Police here. Call me asap.*

Rachel caught Molly as she was about to hit the ground.

# Chapter 8

MOLLY RUBBED HER EYES and blinked them open. What the hell had happened?

"Hey, there," Rachel said. "Slow, okay? You passed out."

"I...Why...Brad," Molly said. The words she needed wouldn't come out. "Is Brad?"

Rachel rubbed Molly's back and said, "I'm so sorry, honey. He's gone. After you passed out, I called Trish. She said it was horrible and not to come down to the hospital. The police had the place on lockdown."

Molly started to cry.

"But how? Why would someone murder him?" Molly said.

"The police are working on it."

"Are they sure it's him? We all wear the same scrubs. Could it be a different doctor? It must be a mistake," Molly said, her voice quivering.

Rachel hugged Molly in a tight embrace. "I'm so sorry. I'm so sorry."

Molly made a whimpering sound, which turned into heaving sobs. All Rachel could do was comfort her friend.

Rachel packed up the ornaments and tablecloth. Molly sat, still in a daze.

"I'm going to bring these to the car. Are you okay here by yourself for a minute?" Rachel asked Molly.

Molly gave a small nod. A single tear ran down her cheek.

On the way home, Molly didn't say a word. Only Rachel knew she and Brad were dating. It was going to be difficult going back to work, even though she and Brad didn't work the same shifts. Sadness washed over her repeatedly. It was in her bones, her muscles, her skin, her heart.

She and Brad had made plans for the following Friday. They rented a house on the beach and had reservations at the iconic beachfront restaurant "World Famous." Molly's heart screamed at the thought of not being able to spend time with Brad ever again. She wanted to claw at the walls and kick at the ground like a two-year-old having a temper tantrum. Most of all, she wanted to find the bastard who killed Brad.

Rachel assisted Molly with getting into her pajamas. She made Molly a cup of her favorite tea, and as they sat at Molly's kitchen table, Rachel held her friend's hand.

"Have a few sips of that, okay?" Rachel said, pointing to the mug.

Although Molly felt like a zombie, she did as Rachel said. She took a sip of the vanilla chamomile tea, but it had no taste. She looked up at Rachel and shook her head.

"I want to call someone," Molly said.

"Who?"

"Someone who can help us figure out why Brad was killed. Do you think it was one of our own? Another doctor or nurse? Or maybe a patient from the psych ward. Did they make sure all the patients were accounted for?"

"Honey, let's get you into bed, okay? It's been a long day," Rachel said.

"Thanks, Rach. I'll be fine. You should get back home to Patrick," Molly said, standing and putting the almost full mug of tea in the sink.

But Molly wouldn't be fine. Not for a long time.

# Chapter 9

GRIEF WAS A FEELING like no other. It was almost impossible to describe, and everyone dealt with grief a little differently. They also reacted to grief differently. For Molly, the wave of sadness was like a film stuck to every inch of her body 24/7. Then came the layer of anger. This layer gave her the energy to get out of bed to find out who killed Brad. This was the layer that allowed her to compartmentalize the sadness and go back to work.

"Molly, it's good to see you. The CEO said if we need to take time off, the hospital will allow it. A few of the nurses have taken the week off," Trish said.

Molly nodded. Although Brad was dead, she still couldn't tell her coworkers that they had been dating. Although it didn't break the hospital code of ethics, she didn't want everyone knowing her business. On top of that, there was a murderer out there. If they knew she and Brad had been together, she might be the next victim.

"Hey, Trish," Molly said. "I'm okay. I see the hospital hired extra security guards. I'm glad they're taking Dr. Mills' death seriously."

Trish nodded.

All day, Molly was hyperaware of what was happening around her. She paid attention to conversations, the people who came in and out of the ER, and if anyone was somewhere he or she shouldn't have been. Everything seemed normal except for the grey cloud that hung over each employee who had worked with Brad. Even Elena, a nurse who didn't particularly like Dr. Mills, said he didn't deserve to be killed.

"I enjoyed working with Dr. Mills," Norma, a senior nurse who worked closely with Brad, said to Molly one evening. "I'm sure you've heard a few of the nurses complain about him. But between you and me, I think it was because they had a crush on him and didn't like his answer when he turned them down."

Molly was surprised at Norma's candid rhetoric. Was that why there were rumors of Brad being difficult to work with? It made perfect sense. Brad had been nothing but a gentleman to Molly.

"Norma, was Brad, I mean, Dr. Mills ever unprofessional? I never had the chance to work with him."

Norma looked up at Molly. "No. He was a good man. And an even better doctor. He was so young to be a trauma surgeon, and I think sometimes he thought he was in over his head. Dr. Mills was attentive to each of his patients. Every one of them."

Molly wanted to respond, but the words were caught in her throat. Instead, she nodded and walked away before the tears started.

That evening, three people—a man and two women—who were involved in a kitchen fire at a Mexican restaurant were admitted. One of the women brought in had been unconscious. The other two were wheezing and having a difficult time breathing.

"Easy one for you, Molly," Luke said, adjusting the man's oxygen mask.

"Thanks, Luke," Molly said. "I'll take over from here."

Molly put all three of the people in the large trauma bay and started each of them with fluids.

"Code blue! Code blue!" a man shouted.

Molly rushed out. A pregnant woman in respiratory arrest was being wheeled in. The right side of her face was badly bruised.

"We've got a thirty-three-year-old female. Thirty-six weeks pregnant. Fell down the stairs at home. Her husband found her unconscious about twenty minutes ago. Breathing is shallow."

Molly followed the gurney into a trauma bay.

"Is she going to be okay?" the husband asked.

"We're going to do our best, okay?" Molly said. "Right now, we need you to go to the front desk and fill out the forms for your wife."

The man nodded and yelled out, "I love you, Dawn. I'll be right here, baby."

"Someone page Dr. Adler," Molly said.

"I'm here," a tall, dark-haired man said. "I'm Kevin Morrison from Mercy. Here to help."

Molly nodded. She had never met this doctor before. After Brad's death, several doctors and nurses from San Diego General went on leave. Surrounding hospitals helped by sending their staff to fill in.

"Dr. Morrison, I'm Nurse Fisher," Molly said as she prepped the patient. Trish came into the room to assist.

"Okay, BP is stable. 118 over 78. Heart rate is good. Breathing is good," he said, moving his stethoscope to the mother's pregnant belly. "Baby's heart rate is good."

"We need to check for internal bleeding," Dr. Morrison said. "Let's start with an ultrasound and do a blood draw."

Art wheeled the machinery over to the doctor.

"If you don't need me anymore, I'm going to check on the other patients," Molly said.

Dr. Morrison gave her a nod and said, "Thank you, Nurse Fisher. Great job in here today. I think we've got it."

Molly cleaned herself up and headed back to the neighboring trauma bay, where she had left the three smoke inhalation victims. Upon opening the curtain, she observed one woman with her eyes closed. The patient's monitor had been turned off. Molly rushed to turn it back. She looked down. The patient was no longer connected to the machine. Molly grabbed the woman's arm to check for a pulse. There was none. She looked at the two other patients in the room. The man's breaths were shallow, and the other woman didn't look as if she was breathing at all. Both of their monitors had also been disconnected and turned off. Who would have done this?

"Linda! Linda!" Molly shouted as she plugged the man's machine back in. Linda ran over. "Who did this?"

The two women were dead—the man, in critical condition.

"Let's get him down to ICU," Linda said.

Who unplugged the machines? Was it the same person who murdered Brad?

# Chapter 10

"MOLLY! MOLLY!"

Molly turned and saw Rachel running to her.

"Hey, Rach. How's it going? Are you off too?"

"I have three more hours. What are you doing tonight?"

Molly shrugged. It had been two weeks since Brad's murder, and the police still didn't have any leads.

"Nothing. I was going to pick up a burger and shake from Jerry's and head home. Top Chef awaits."

"Hey, listen, so our hospital is in the lead for most donor sign-ups and most donors this year. A few of us are going to Altitude this evening. Why don't you come? My sister is spending the night with Patrick."

Molly looked at her friend and wrinkled her nose. She didn't want to do anything for the past two weeks but stay inside. Brad would have been appalled by her collection of takeout containers and pizza boxes.

"C'mon, Molly. You can't stay in and sulk for the rest of your life. Brad wouldn't have wanted that. Just one drink. Maybe two. Trish,

Art, and Linda are coming. And that doctor who helped a few weeks ago? Morrison? I think he and Trish have something going on."

"Really? Good for her. That girl is a workaholic," Molly said. "Okay, maybe I'll come out for a bit. What time?"

"I'll pick you up at nine," Rachel said and ran back toward the hospital.

Molly slid a simple, black dress over her head. She touched the necklace that hung around her neck, a simple gold charm with an "M." Brad had given it to her on their third date. Molly took a deep breath and whispered, "I miss you."

The doorbell rang. Molly slid on her black leather ballet flats and opened the door. Rachel was wearing a blue sequin top and a short black skirt. Her six-inch heels made Molly's feet hurt just looking at them.

"Wow," Molly said. "Look at you. I'm like a street mouse next to your bling-bling."

"Oh, stop. You're not getting out of it that easily. Plus, you look great," Rachel said, pulling Molly out the front door.

The Altitude Sky Lounge was a popular venue, with its panoramic views and handcrafted cocktails. Trish, Art, Linda, and Dr. Morrison were standing at a high-top table. Trish's head was thrown back as she laughed at whatever Dr. Morrison had said.

"Hey!" Rachel said as she and Molly made their way over.

"It turns out doctors and nurses clean up pretty good, don't you think?" Linda said, in her fuchsia pink sheath dress and faux fur shawl.

"Damn right!" Rachel said. "We deserve to have a little fun without the scrubs."

"And blood," Molly added.

Dr. Morrison laughed. "Good one. We sure live different lives from other folks. So, how have things been at SD? Did they ever catch the guy who killed Dr. Mills?"

Molly's heart fluttered. She had to remind herself not to react to comments like this. She had done a great job of not falling apart at work for the past two weeks. Rachel grabbed Molly's hand and squeezed.

"Uh, no. But let's not talk about it. It's not a pleasant subject," Rachel said.

"Of course," Dr. Morrison said. "How insensitive of me. He was your coworker and friend. I apologize."

Molly turned to Rachel. "Let's get a drink."

Rachel nodded.

"Anyone need anything?" The group shook their heads, and Molly and Rachel made their way to the bar.

"Thanks," Molly said. "Although it's been two weeks, I almost lost it when Dr. Morrison said Brad's name."

"I've got your back," Rachel said, wrapping her arm around Molly.

"And I've got yours," Molly said, holding her Cosmopolitan up to Rachel's.

As they made their way back to the table, Rachel and Molly noticed an additional attendee.

"Dr. Adler!" Rachel said. "What a surprise."

"Rachel," Dr. Adler said. "It's so nice to see you. All of you. What a great idea."

Dr. Adler reached across the table to shake Dr. Morrison's hand. "I don't believe we've met. David Adler, Chief of Trauma, SD General."

Dr. Morrison shook Dr. Adler's hand. "Kevin Morrison, Trauma Team Leader over at Mercy."

The group chatted about everything from first-year residency to NFL football.

"Chargers looked good this year," Dr. Morrison said. "Are you all San Diego natives?"

They all nodded except for Linda.

"I am from Colombia. My parents came to the U.S. when I was seven years old," Linda said. "So even though I wasn't born here, I consider San Diego to be my home."

Dr. Morrison nodded.

"I'm more of a Forty-Niners fan myself," Dr. Adler said, at which he was playfully booed by the others at the table.

Molly chuckled. Brad had grown up a Los Angeles Raiders fan. That was before they moved back to Oakland in 1995, right after Brad had graduated from high school. If he were standing at the table with them, she wondered if he would get booed as well. Molly's throat caught, and she took a sip of water. Leaning over to Rachel, she said, "I'm going to use the restroom. Be right back."

Molly headed to the main bar area in search of the ladies' room. After washing her hands and inspecting her makeup, she headed back to the table. As she opened the door to the restroom, a hand reached out, gently grabbing her arm.

"Molly!" a hushed voice said.

Startled, Molly turned around. It was a face she would recognize anywhere.

# Chapter 11

"DR. NELSON!" MOLLY SAID. "What are you doing here?"

Dr. Nelson was the obstetrician who delivered her as a baby. He was the first pair of hands to have ever held her. Molly remembered tagging along on her mother's doctor's appointments when she was a little girl and sitting in the waiting room. Mrs. Nelson, the doctor's wife, was his receptionist and always had fun activities for Molly to do—from coloring to card games. Afterwards, Dr. Nelson came out to say hello and give her a lollipop. Her mom later told Molly that Dr. Nelson had treated her like the daughter he never had. When Molly's mom didn't have health insurance, Dr. Nelson took care of her. Now, the fragile old man standing in front of her looked like a shell of the vibrant doctor she once knew. Regardless, Molly saw Dr. Nelson as a man she could trust.

"Molly, I need you to listen to me. We don't have much time," Dr. Nelson said.

"Dr. Nelson. What a wonderful surprise," Molly said, then registered his words. "What's wrong? Why are you here?"

"Have you heard of the Luna Foundation?"

"No, I don't think so," Molly said. She sensed the urgency in Dr. Nelson's face.

"They're attempting to get as many people to sign up for organ donation as possible," he said. "Hospitals are being promised large dollar amounts."

"Oh, right. I think I saw a flyer in the breakroom about the program. Organ donation helps thousands of people each year, Dr. Nelson."

"Right. Of course it does. But there's something not right about this program."

"Isn't it a good thing to have as many people sign up for organ donation as we can?"

"Molly. I received a call. I can't tell you who from, but this person told me doctors and nurses are being killed, and it's linked to this foundation."

"I don't understand, Dr. Nelson."

"The Luna Foundation is sponsoring some kind of contest. Look into it," Dr. Nelson said.

"I don't understand. Why would the hospital partner with a company if it were doing something unethical?"

"I don't have the details, Molly. Please research the foundation but be discreet. And Molly, don't trust anyone."

"Molly! There you are!" Rachel's voice called out.

"I'll be in touch," Dr. Nelson said.

Molly looked up, and the old man was gone. What had he just told her? And why was he back here, in San Diego? Dr. Nelson had retired. He had to be in his late eighties by now. Molly hadn't seen him in over 18 years.

# Chapter 12

"YOU SAW WHO?" RACHEL asked, her words slightly slurred.

"Never mind," Molly said. "It's nothing."

"I have to pee," Rachel said, bending down to take her heels off. "These shoes are killing me."

Molly stopped her friend from taking off her shoes in the restroom hallway.

"Here, let's trade," Molly said, propping her drunk friend up against the wall to swap shoes.

It wasn't an easy feat trading shoes with a drunk woman. But Molly realized it was nothing compared to walking in Rachel's shoes. She silently cursed her best friend for wearing six-inch stilettos.

As Molly and Rachel made their way back to the table, Linda looked at them with a sobering stare. In fact, everyone at the table looked as if someone had died.

"What's wrong, Linda?" Molly asked.

"Norma's dead. She was murdered."

Molly lay in bed, listening to the sound of Rachel's snores. How could Norma be dead? She had worked at SD General for over twenty years. Who would want to hurt her? The same people who killed Brad, that's who. Molly was aware there would be other deaths if she didn't uncover the meaning of all of this. She thought about what Dr. Nelson had told her. Was the organ donor program linked to Brad and Norma's deaths? But how? Molly tossed and turned all night trying to connect the dots.

# Chapter 13

"Molly, scalpel," Dr. Adler commanded.

Molly handed him the instrument and observed as he made a small incision near the young man's belly button. The laparoscopy was a simple procedure that would show Dr. Adler where the bullet was lodged. There was no exit hole, and the point of entry was close to the patient's appendix.

"Oh, that smells bad," Molly said, hovering the back of her hand near her face mask.

"We've got a ruptured appendix. We need to remove it, or he could die," Dr. Adler said. "Molly, get me a drainage tube."

Molly did as the doctor asked. Art monitored the patient's vitals.

Dr. Adler took twenty minutes to remove the young man's appendix, suturing the incisions neatly. The patient was lucky he was brought to the hospital in time.

Dr. Adler and Molly washed up at the scrub station.

"I'm impressed, Molly. You've been getting more confident in the operating room. You're less hesitant. Less nervous," Dr. Adler said.

"Thank you, doctor. I owe it all to you. I've observed how calm and collected you are in every situation. I hope to be like that someday," Molly said.

Three hours and eight patients later, with no injuries worse than a frying pan burn, Molly changed into her street clothes. She pulled out her hair tie and let out a deep sigh.

"Long day, huh?" Trish said.

"Yeah. Not too bad, though. You off?"

"Uh huh. And I have three days off in a row."

"Lucky," Molly said. "You deserve it, though, Trish. I don't know how you do it."

"Me neither," Trish chuckled.

"So, are you and Dr. Morrison a thing now?" Molly asked, a pang of jealousy striking her from out of nowhere.

"We're getting there. I like him a lot. I took the time off for a weekend getaway," Trish said. "Can I ask you something?"

"Sure," Molly said, zipping her duffel bag closed.

"How did you do it?"

"Do what?"

"How did you date a surgeon? I find it so difficult with our random schedules and long hours," Trish said.

Molly put her hand over her mouth, then whispered, "You knew?"

"Well, of course, silly. Every time you walked by him at the end of your shift, your eyes did this little smiley thing," Trish said. "Oh, but don't worry. I don't think anyone else noticed. I stare at faces all day, so I'm pretty good at reading expressions."

It made sense. Trish worked the front desk a lot. The only time she worked the floor was when Dr. Adler needed her or if the ER became inundated with patients.

"We spent every moment that we could together. He mostly came over to my place since I'm so close to downtown. Our schedules were so opposite, I don't think we ever had a full day off together."

"That's what I mean. It's tough," Trish said, closing her locker. "Thanks, Molly."

Trish walked over to Molly and hugged her. "And I'm sorry about what happened. Dr. Mills was a good guy."

Molly's heart sank a little. The thoughts of what her life would have been like with Brad flooded her brain. She shut her eyes and took a deep breath.

# Chapter 14

MOLLY PICKED THROUGH THE crochet critters that hadn't sold at the bazaar. She remembered being so excited to have her own table and showcase the cute ornaments she and Rachel had spent hours making. But that was the day her world fell apart. That was the day Brad was murdered.

Molly slid her laptop out from its case, opened a browser window, and typed in "Luna Foundation." From the outside, it presented as a legitimate company that owned several prestigious hospitals in California. As Molly dug deeper, she observed a few oddities. For one thing, the photos on their website for the Board of Directors didn't exactly look real. From first glance, sure, they were headshots of smiling faces. But as Molly zoomed in on each one, there were missing ears or an odd lump, a face that had a small chunk taken out of it, and so on. Are these fake people? Either that, or they were poorly Photoshopped.

Molly Googled the first man's name—Edward Braylen. Nothing came up other than the Luna website. She searched LinkedIn and

Facebook. Nothing. The woman next to him, Cynthia Chang, came up with similar results. One by one, Molly researched each name. None of them had any information other than what was on the Luna Foundation website.

She looked up the company on the Better Business Bureau. Not found. She scrolled to the bottom of the website page. The company address was in Burbank, California. She did a Google Maps search and ended up at a warehouse in industrial Burbank. Wouldn't a business need to be registered? Molly typed the business name into the California Secretary of State website. Not found. This business was a fake. But who was behind it?

Molly Googled "Ronald Nelson." Several listings came up, so she narrowed the search to "Ronald Nelson, San Diego." It was nothing but old articles about Dr. Nelson, his patients, and his practice. She read an article about his retirement in 1991. Laurelville. That's where he and his wife moved to. It was a tiny town south of San Diego. Molly Googled, "Ronald Nelson, Laurelville." There it was: "Ronald and Virginia Nelson, Laurelville, California. Phone (555) 743-1313."

The phone rang five times before a voice came on the line.

"Hello?" an older woman's voice said.

"Oh, hello, is this the Nelson residence?" Molly asked.

"It is. Who is this?"

"My name is Molly. Is this Ginny? I'm not sure if you remember me, but…"

"Oh, dear, yes, of course. My gin rummy partner. You used to come into Ronald's office with your mother when you were a wee girl. How are you?"

"I'm doing okay. It's nice to hear your voice."

"Here, let me find out what the doctor is up to. I'm sure he'll be ecstatic to receive your call."

There was a brief pause with some shuffling in the background, and a man's voice came on the line.

"Molly?"

"Hi, Dr. Nelson. I'm sorry to bother you like this," Molly said.

"No, no, it's no bother. Did you think about what I told you, Molly? Did you find out more?"

"A nurse is dead now. One of the senior nurses. I researched the Luna Foundation, and it doesn't look legitimate. I couldn't find anything online except that it is in Burbank, California."

"I see. Molly, you may be in grave danger. Tell the hospital you need time off and go stay with your mother. I'll contact you when I find out more. Please stay safe and watch your back. Do you understand me?"

"Yes, yes, I understand."

Molly started her shift with one goal in mind—to find out more about the Luna Foundation without getting caught. She knew running away wasn't the answer.

"Hey, Trish!" she said. "What's on the menu today?"

"Hey, Moll. Just your usual. The kid in bay 2 fell off his skateboard. The pregnant woman in bay 3 had food poisoning, but we're getting ready to discharge her after giving her fluids and stopping the nausea. Other than that, it's been quiet."

"Music to my ears," Molly said. "Trish, you've heard about that organ donation campaign, right?"

"Sure," Trish said. "The doctors are really pushing in. Here's the flyer they're circulating if you want to know more."

Molly took the flyer from Trish and scanned it.

"Give the gift of life. Become an organ donor today."

The flyer emphasized the importance of organ donation and its potential impact on the lives of others.

"What about the contest?" Molly asked.

"Oh, you heard about that? It's not a formal contest. At least, that's what I was told. Some of the doctors decided to do a friendly competition to see who could get the most signups. Supposedly, it's for bragging rights only."

"Hmm," Molly said. Maybe Dr. Nelson was wrong about the organ donation program. But how would he have found out about it all the way in Laurelville? There had to be more to this. She would have to ask around without getting caught.

As Molly restocked the first aid drawer in trauma bay one, she noticed the large gauze pads were running low. She made her way down the corridor to the supply closet but stopped in her tracks when the sound of whispers came from the janitorial closet.

"...stop her," the voice whispered. "Promise me...won't get hurt."

"You saw what happened...Mills...Norma. You don't want..." the other voice whispered. "Do what they..."

"Okay, just promise..." the other voice said.

The door handle opened, and Molly turned the corner. She peeked around the bend. Coming out of the closet was Rachel. Her best friend scurried down the hall. But who had she been talking to? Molly waited, but no one else appeared. What should she do? Open the door to the janitorial closet? She stood for a minute contemplating her next move.

"What are you doing?"

Molly jumped a mile. Luke, the EMT, was standing behind her. He laughed.

"Are you okay, Miss Molly?" he said. "Looks like you just saw a ghost."

"Oh, hey, Luke. No, I was trying to remember what supplies I needed to refill the trauma bay. What brings you in? Was there a code I missed?"

Molly kept her eyes glued to the janitor's closet door. She didn't want to miss whoever was in there.

"I'm here for a transport. Bay 4," he said, shrugging.

"Mm, gotcha," Molly said. "Okay, well, good to see you, Luke. Happy holidays."

"Happy holidays, Molly. Say, would you like to go for a drink or dinner sometime?"

This took Molly by surprise. Her eyes moved from the closet door to Luke's. In the last year she had known Luke, she never thought of him that way. Clearly, he did, though. After Brad, Molly didn't think she was ready to date again. Sure, she and Brad had only been together for a month, but she would be scarred by his death forever.

"Umm," Molly said.

Luke's face turned red.

"I mean, it's okay if you don't want to," Luke said, trying to play it cool.

"It's not that. I recently got out of a relationship and I'm not sure I'm ready to date again," Molly explained.

"Sure, I understand," Luke said. "It's totally fine. You seem like a sweet person. Thought I'd ask."

"Thanks, Luke," Molly said. "I think you're great, too. Maybe one day."

With that, Luke and Molly said goodbye and went on their way. Molly had almost forgotten about the closet door. She walked to the janitor's closet and threw open the door. Empty. Had the person left while she was talking to Luke? She had to find Rachel.

"Hey, Rach. Trish and I are ordering sushi. Want anything? My treat," Molly asked her friend.

She wasn't sure how to bring up the whole closet conversation yet.

Rachel looked up from the clipboard she was holding.

"Umm, no. I think I'll get a breath of fresh air during lunch. Clear my head. Thanks, though," Rachel said.

Molly nodded. and clicked the "place order" button on her app. She hoped Rachel was okay. It was unlike her friend to say no to sushi.

"Food should be here in thirty minutes," she told Trish, who was on the phone and answered with a thumbs up.

What was Rachel up to? A breath of fresh air? Rachel hated being outdoors. The sushi arrived ten minutes early, and as Molly ate her last piece of shrimp tempura roll, she had an idea.

"Hey, Trish? Could I borrow your car for a minute? I need to pick something up, and my car is in the shop," Molly said.

Trish threw Molly the keys to her Dodge Charger, and Molly slipped out the back door of the hospital. Rachel had clocked out, and if Molly timed it correctly, she could follow her friend.

Molly sat in Trish's car, ignition off. She was glad Trish's windows were tinted and slid down in the seat to make sure Rachel couldn't see her.

Five minutes passed. No Rachel. Each time Molly saw the hospital door open, she caught a little surge of adrenaline. A man in a long wool overcoat exited the hospital. He was wearing sunglasses. Was that Dr. Adler? Molly squinted her eyes. It was.

Dr. Adler climbed into a Porsche 911, the next row over.

The hospital door opened once again. Rachel.

Molly watched as Rachel climbed into Dr. Adler's car and they drove off. Was Rachel having an affair with a married man? And was he the person Rachel was speaking to in the closet? Molly started the Charger and followed them.

# Chapter 15

DR. ADLER AND RACHEL ordered meals at Vitorio's Italian Restaurant. So far, their actions hadn't led her to believe they were in a romantic relationship. When the meal was finished, Dr. Adler put his credit card on the tray. He then did something that Molly didn't expect. He pulled out a manila folder and slid it across the table to Rachel. Rachel gasped, then closed the folder. Dr. Adler reached across the table and squeezed Rachel's hand. What was going on?

Rachel opened the folder back up. She took a deep, heaving breath, looked up at Dr. Adler, and nodded.

Molly had seen all she wanted to at the restaurant. As she walked past the nurses' station, she handed Trish's keys back to her.

"Everything okay?" Trish asked.

"Sure, yeah. Thanks for letting me borrow your car," Molly said.

"Anytime," Trish said, her eyes focused on her computer screen. From the corner of her eye, she saw Dr. Adler and Rachel come in through the hospital side door.

# Chapter 16

MOLLY CALLED AN UBER to bring her to her mechanic's shop. Her Ford Mustang, Fred, had received new brakes and had his fluids changed. Her mechanic, Sam, took good care of Fred, and she made a mental note to bring something nice to Sam for Christmas.

A white Toyota Camry pulled up, and she matched the license plate to that of her Uber app.

"Hi, there, Molly?" the driver said.

Molly nodded and slid into the passenger's seat. She put her seatbelt on, and the driver proceeded on the route. Molly sat back and relaxed, closing her eyes for a minute.

When she opened them, which seemed like only a minute later, they were nowhere near her mechanic's shop.

"Where are we?" Molly asked.

"I need to make one quick stop before going to your destination. It will only take a few more minutes," the driver said.

Inside, Molly was getting increasingly irritated. When she ordered the ride, the app didn't show that any other riders would be picked up along the way.

The car stopped in an alley in downtown San Diego. Molly looked around but didn't see anyone. She turned to the driver, who, oddly enough, was looking straight ahead down the alley. Molly followed his gaze. There, walking toward her, was a large, burly man the size of an NFL player. Molly's heart skipped a beat, and before she could process what was going on, the driver had unlocked the car doors, and the man was opening her door.

"Wait," she said, as the man reached across to unbuckle her seatbelt. "What's going on?"

"Ms. Fisher?" the man said. "There's someone who would like to speak with you. Please come with me."

Molly sat, dumbfounded.

"And if I don't?" she asked.

"Please don't make this more difficult than it needs to be."

Molly looked again at the driver, who still had no expression.

"I need you to take me to my mechanic," Molly said. "I don't know what you're trying to pull here, but I'm not getting out of the car."

The driver did not move. Instead, the man standing at Molly's open door grabbed her arm and pulled her out of the car as if she were a rag doll.

Molly screamed as the man threw her over his shoulder. The driver handed the man Molly's duffel bag and took off. She kicked as hard as she could, but her efforts were useless.

The man entered a steel door in the alleyway and closed it behind him with a thud. He set Molly down on a chair.

"Stay there. And don't try to leave. No one will hear you if you scream," the man said.

He went through a back door, and Molly stood, looking at the door through which they had come in. She ran over to it and pushed. It was no use. The door was either too heavy, or it was locked. There were no windows in the room, only a small, empty shelving unit. What was this place?

The back door opened, and Molly stood up from the chair. A man who looked familiar walked into the room.

"Hello, Molly," Dr. Morrison said. "Remember me?"

# Chapter 17

MOLLY WAS AT A loss for words.

"Dr. Morrison? What are you doing here? Why am I here?" Molly asked.

"Molly, I need you to listen to me. Brad and Norma's deaths weren't random," Dr. Morrison said.

"Well, yeah, I realize that. They were murdered," Molly said. "Who did it? And why?"

"You know about the organ donor drive," he continued. "There's an organization that is pushing doctors to kill patients so that they can harvest the patients' organs."

"But that's not possible. That's unethical. It goes against the Hippocratic Oath," Molly said.

"It's why Brad and Norma were murdered."

"What? For their organs?"

"No, because they wouldn't go along with the program. And they spoke their minds. They refused to assist in killing patients," Dr.

Morrison said. "In not so many words, they told the CEO of the Luna Foundation to fuck off. Brad reported them to the hospital board."

"What...what about you? What about Dr. Ad..." Molly dropped off as she realized what was going on.

"Believe me. I've been watching my back."

Molly was starting to put the pieces of the puzzle together. Dr. Adler's justification of the obese woman's death now made sense. The patients under Dr. Adler's care who died were the ones he decided could be sacrificed because they had done something wrong in his eyes. Jose, the man who was cheating on his wife; Mrs. Stephenson, the morbidly obese woman who refused to lose weight for her own good and was a burden on her son; and the three people in the fire, two of whom were here without visas. Dr. Adler hadn't wanted to kill people or play God, but the only way for him not to meet the same demise as Brad was to go along with the Luna Foundation's plans.

"What about me?" Molly asked. "Is someone after me?"

"We don't know yet," Dr. Morrison said. "But following Dr. Adler is not a good idea."

"How did you find out about that? And who's we?"

"Trish and me. You borrowed Trish's car today. Trish knows where Dr. Adler's favorite lunch spot is, Molly."

Of course. Trish's car had location tracking. It made sense.

"So, what do we do?"

"I put in for a transfer to another state. Trish did the same. I suggest you follow suit."

"But what about Rachel? And Dr. Adler? What about all the other doctors and nurses who may lose their lives?" Molly said in horror. "Running away won't solve anything."

"I don't have another solution. This thing is bigger than we are."

"We need to fight. You said Brad reported the foundation to the board. What did the board say?"

Dr. Morrison looked at Molly sorrowfully and said, "They're the ones who ordered the hit. The foundation is paying the hospital big bucks for these organs, Molly."

# Chapter 18

DECEMBER 2009 CHRISTMAS DAY

Molly sat in her mother Dena's living room, a steaming cup of tea in her hands. It was Christmas, and her original plans had been to bring Brad to meet Dena and Dena's boyfriend, Rob. Christmas music played on the stereo, and Dena had turned on the TV to display the Yuletide Log, a tradition that she and Molly had ever since Molly was little. Christmas had always been such a happy time for them.

"Honey? Are you okay?" Dena asked, walking in with a tray of freshly baked cookies. "You're awfully quiet."

Molly looked up at her mother—the woman who had raised her and would give her the world if she asked for it. Growing up without a father had not been ideal, and Dena never gave Molly a straight answer when she asked about him. Her father was a doctor but left town before Molly was born.

"Yeah, Mom. Sorry. I guess I was off in my own little world," Molly said.

Dena sat next to her daughter and wrapped her arms around Molly.

"You know you can tell me anything," Dena said.

A knock on the door sounded, and Dena jumped up.

"That must be Rob," Dena said.

A large man, highly resembling a lumberjack, followed Dena into the room. Molly almost laughed because he reminded her so much of the Claymation lumberjack character from Frosty the Snowman with his red beanie, red beard and mustache, and jolly expression. Molly stood and put out her hand. Instead, Rob opened his arms, inviting a hug. Molly laughed and stepped forward into the giant's arms. She let out a giggle, and he a hearty laugh.

"It's good to meet you, kiddo. Your mom has told me so much about you, I feel as if I already know you," Rob said, releasing her from his bear hug.

There was something about Rob's energy that gave Molly a rush of cheerfulness. It was as if his jolliness was contagious. No wonder her mom liked him so much.

"It's nice to meet you, too, Rob," Molly said. "I'm so glad we could get together."

Rob removed his coat and beanie and turned to Dena.

"Shall I get started in the kitchen?" Rob asked.

Dena nodded. "Everything is all set and ready to go. Have at it, sweetie."

Rob kissed Dena and headed into the kitchen.

"Wow, he cooks too?" Molly said. "Impressive."

"I think so, too," Dena said, winking at Molly. "So, back to you. Tell me what's on your mind. Even as a little girl, you had that expression when you were deep in thought."

Molly told Dena about Dr. Nelson and his warning. She also told Dena about her encounter with Dr. Morrison.

Dena looked down at the floor and shook her head. She whispered to herself, "No, no, no. This can't be happening."

"Mama? What can't be happening? Tell me," Molly said.

"Your father is back."

"My father? What do you mean he's back?" Molly asked.

As Molly listened closely to what Dena revealed, she realized her mother had spent her whole life protecting her.

Molly's father was a man named Abraham Nelson. Born to Ronald and Virginia Nelson, Abraham was a well-known doctor in the San Diego area until he was accused of stealing money from the hospital where he worked in the form of bogus charities. Abraham had created a charity for everything from childhood cancer to drug addiction. He had siphoned money through these charities that went straight into his pocket. Dena was unaware of Abraham's doings at the time, but later, when the police came knocking at her door, everything came to light. By that time, Abraham had packed his things and disappeared. As far as Dena knew, no one, not even his parents, had been in contact with him. With the Luna Foundation coming to light, Dena had a strong suspicion that her ex-husband was behind it.

Molly looked at her mother in horror. Her father was a criminal. The Nelsons were her grandparents. No wonder they looked after her and her mother so carefully. They carried a deep sense of guilt for what their son had done. A mix of emotions filled Molly—anger at her mother for not telling her, anger at her father for being a criminal, and sadness that all this time she never knew the kind couple at the doctor's office were her grandparents.

"Please don't be mad at me," Dena said. "I was trying to protect you. Dr. Nelson and I believed it was better for you to live your own life and not in the shadow of your criminal father."

"I understand why you did it, Mom. But I wish you had told me sooner," Molly said. "Now, where can we find him?"

"It's not safe, Molly. Your father is a different man than the one I fell in love with almost thirty years ago," Dena said. "Promise me you won't do anything to put yourself in danger."

# Chapter 19

DECEMBER 2009 NEW YEAR'S EVE

"Happy Almost 2010!" Rachel said as she handed Molly a glass of champagne.

"Hey, Rach. Thanks for having me. Work has been kicking my ass," Molly said. "I'm grateful to have a day off. Do you ever notice that the number of illnesses and accidents goes up during the winter months? Every day is another game of rotating patients."

"Yep, I hear you there, sister. I'm glad we got that new trauma surgeon in. Things were getting tight there for a minute."

Molly sat down at Rachel's kitchen table, sipping her champagne. Pushing aside a few of the papers scattered on the table, her eyes rest on a bill sitting on top. San Diego Medical Center Pharmacy, $3209.

"Rach?" Molly asked. "Are you doing okay with finances?"

Rachel's son, Patrick, had recently been diagnosed with type 1 diabetes. Rachel was stressed about the medical bills pouring in. Being a single mom wasn't easy, and with Rachel's mom gone, Rachel was more alone than ever. Rachel's sister came to help when she could, but she had her own family and lived over an hour away.

"Oh, that," she said. "It's been paid. I was behind a few months on Patrick's insulin, but it's been taken care of. Thanks for asking, though. It was getting rough there for a few months, but I was able to catch up on bills."

"Good, because if you ever need to borrow money, I'm here for you. No interest at the bank of Molly," Molly said jokingly.

Rachel held her glass out to Molly's and clinked them together. "Thank you for being the best friend a girl could have. I mean that. I love you, Molls."

"Keep the change, you filthy animal," Patrick said, laughing, then turned to Rachel. "Mama, I'm hungry."

They had finished watching *Home Alone* for what Rachel thought was the fifth time this month. It was Patrick's favorite movie, and she loved the expressions he made while watching the comedy.

"Okay, what would you like? Ham and cheese roll-ups? Or how about some leftover chili from dinner?"

"Mm, chili, please," Patrick said. "I've got to go potty. Be right back."

"Coming right up." Rachel stood and held her hand out to Molly. "Refill?"

Molly handed Rachel her glass.

"Yes, please. Just a little. I don't want to fall asleep before the ball drops."

Rachel made her way into the kitchen, and Molly grabbed the TV remote. She flipped through a few channels before realizing Rachel had different cable channels than she did.

"Hey, do you have one of those TV cable guide cards?" Molly called out to her friend.

"It should be in the entertainment center cabinet thing. Either that or it's in the magazine rack by the couch," Rachel called to her.

Molly opened the door to the entertainment cabinet. She found a few random items, but no TV card. Turning around, she knelt next to the magazine caddy. As she searched for the card, she saw a manila envelope wedged between a copy of Family Circle and a copy of Glamour. Remembering the manila envelope Dr. Adler gave Rachel the day she followed them, Molly's heart skipped a beat. She looked over her shoulder. Rachel was humming as she took Patrick's chili out of the microwave. Molly quickly slid the folder out from its place and opened it.

The folder contained a letterhead from the Luna Foundation, and Molly quickly recognized the form to be some kind of non-disclosure agreement. She scanned the document and turned the page. And that was when she saw it. A promise of two million dollars made payable to Rachel Banks.

# Chapter 20

JANUARY 2010

On the drive home, Molly felt sick to her stomach. Her boyfriend had been murdered. Her father was a criminal. And now this. Her best friend, the person she thought she could trust, was selling out to a company for two million dollars.

As she pulled onto her street, she saw a man standing near the apartment complex's garage. Although Molly didn't recognize him, her senses told her to drive around the block before pulling into the garage. When she came back around, the man was gone.

Exhausted, Molly walked up the stairs to her apartment. She realized she was being paranoid about everything and everyone around her. But she had every right to be. She couldn't stop thinking about Rachel. Was this the only way her friend could pay for Patrick's medical bills? Certainly not. But having an extra two million dollars in the bank would certainly help. Molly didn't have a chance to read the whole agreement, but she assumed it had to do with the Luna Foundation's organ donor program.

Molly was still thinking about this as she reached the third floor. She turned down the hallway and was met with a pair of blue eyes that were so piercing, she thought she had been stabbed. She knew what she had to do.

Run.

# Chapter 21

JANUARY 2010

As Molly flew down the stairs, adrenaline pumping, she didn't dare look back. A voice called out to her.

"Molly, please, can we talk?"

She gripped her keys, ready to burst into the garage and jump into Fred. Her finger felt around on Fred's key fob and pushed the panic button. Fred blared his alarm, loud and steady. She felt a hand on her shoulder. It squeezed. Tightly. Molly tried to shrug it off, but she was pushed to the ground. Molly screamed. She was ready to fight. Turning onto her back, Molly covered her face with one forearm and kicked her perpetrator. The man stumbled backward.

"I just want to talk," the man said.

The man looked oddly familiar, and as Molly realized why, she felt ill.

"You. You're my father. Abraham Nelson," Molly said.

"That's right. Molly, I've waited so long to meet you," Abraham said.

"Why are you here? What do you want from me?"

The man stayed where he was. Molly slowly stood up and brushed herself off. He put his hands up in a truce.

"I need your help, Molly. I'm not sure what your mother told you about me, but I'm a good man. Like you, I save lives. I want to work together to save even more lives."

"No, you scam people for your own benefit," Molly said. "I don't want any part of that."

The man's expression changed. Molly saw the anger as it took over his body. She started backpedaling toward Fred. Abraham started moving toward her.

"Don't you understand? You're my daughter. My flesh and blood. I want to share this with you. And your mother. She raised you well. A nurse, just like her," Abraham said.

"I don't want it. Please leave," Molly said.

Abraham sped up his pace, and Molly turned to run. She screamed again. Abraham tackled her to the ground. Molly struggled. He placed his hand over her mouth.

"Shh, not so fast," Abraham said. "You're coming with me."

The garage door opened. A car door slammed, followed by the sound of feet running. She struggled under Abraham's weight as she turned on her back. A pair of work boots came into her line of sight, followed by navy blue pants. And suddenly, Abraham was no longer on top of her. Molly scrambled to her feet. She looked up and saw Abraham pinned up against the wall, his wrists zip-tied. Then, she looked into the eyes of the man who had saved her from an unknown fate—Luke.

# Chapter 22

JANUARY 2021

Molly took the patient's blood pressure and wrote the information on the woman's chart. She headed up to the front desk, where she told Nurse Marty Hampton that she would be heading out for lunch.

Molly had been working as a nurse at a palliative care clinic in Las Vegas, Nevada, for the past eleven years. After her father was convicted of healthcare fraud and conspiracy, Molly decided she needed a change of scenery. Her mother and Rob were happily married, Rachel moved in with her sister and was able to get out of debt, and Trish and Dr. Morrison had decided to stay in San Diego. Molly and Luke had dated for a few months after the incident but decided they were better off as friends. Molly had visited her grandfather and grandmother several times in the past eleven years, and a special bond had formed. The Nelsons spoiled Molly when she came to visit several times a year.

As Molly walked back in from her lunch break, Marty said, "Perfect timing, Molly. You've got a phone call."

Molly took the phone from Marty.

"Hello?"

"Hi, is this Molly Fisher?"

"It is. Who is this?"

"This is Laurelville General Hospital CEO Scott Barneson. I'm calling because your grandfather has passed peacefully in his sleep. Your grandmother is requesting your transfer to Laurelville as her full-time caregiver."

# Thank you!

Thank you so much for reading Silent Harvest. If you liked this book, get ready for the launch of What the Neighborhood Knows in early 2026. It's a psychological thriller set in Laurelville—the same town Molly relocates to.

Please consider leaving a review on Amazon and/or Goodreads. I would greatly appreciate it. Be sure to subscribe to my email newsletter for free books, book launch updates and announcements, and live events. Visit kristinafox.com for more details.

# About the author

Kristina Fox is a certified personal trainer based in the San Francisco Bay Area, where she combines her passion for wellness with a lifelong love of storytelling. A dedicated reader since the age of three, she brings her deep appreciation for mystery and suspense to her writing. Kristina's favorite pastimes include sipping wine, enjoying sushi, and competing in lively board games—all preferably in the company of family. Mysteries remain her favorite escape.

# Also by the author

Also by Kristina Fox
The Kelsey James Fitness Mystery Series
Candy & Cardio
Time Under Tension
Double Progression
\*\*\*

Standalones
What the Neighborhood Knows

www.ingramcontent.com/pod-product-compliance
Lightning Source LLC
Chambersburg PA
CBHW071202130626
46555CB00004B/1550